Camping with the President

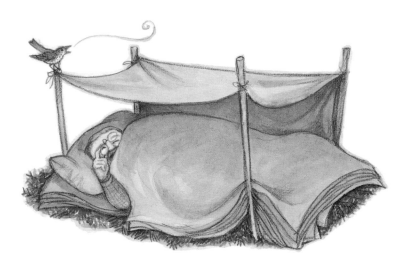

Camping with the President

Ginger Wadsworth

Illustrated by Karen Dugan

CALKINS CREEK
Honesdale, Pennsylvania

In remembrance of Mayme Kimes (1909–2002), jewel of the Sierra Nevada

—*G.W.*

For my wonderful friend Doreen O'Connor, who opened the door to my love
of history with humor and zeal

—*K.D.*

Text copyright © 2009 by Ginger Wadsworth
Illustrations copyright © 2009 by Karen Dugan

Calkins Creek
An Imprint of Boyds Mills Press, Inc.
815 Church Street
Honesdale, Pennsylvania 18431
Printed in China

Library of Congress Cataloging-in-Publication Data

Wadsworth, Ginger.
  Camping with the president / Ginger Wadsworth ; illustrated by Karen Dugan. — 1st ed.
    p. cm.
  Includes bibliographical references.
  ISBN 978-1-59078-497-6 (hardcover : alk. paper)
  1. Roosevelt, Theodore, 1858–1919—Travel—California—Yosemite Valley—Juvenile literature.
2. Muir, John, 1838–1914—Juvenile literature. 3. Yosemite National Park (Calif.)—History—Juvenile
literature. 4. National parks and reserves—United States—History—Juvenile literature.
5. Environmentalism—United States—History—Juvenile literature. I. Dugan, Karen. II. Title.

E757.W137 2009
973.91'1092—dc22

                              2008024155

First edition
The text of this book is set in 13-point Adobe Garamond.
The illustrations are done in watercolor.

10 9 8 7 6 5 4 3 2 1

Makofsky, Rachel

This item needs to be routed to the
Public Holds Shelf.

Barcode: 31254002833677
Title: Camping with the president

Call Number: J OP W

Hold for patron Makofsky, Rachel
Barcode: 21254000694362
Notify by text: 9175206821
Notify by email:
rachel_makofsky@yahoo.com

Request Date: 2/5/2021 9:58 AM
Slip Date: 2/5/2021 11:55 AM
Printed by Circulation at HOL

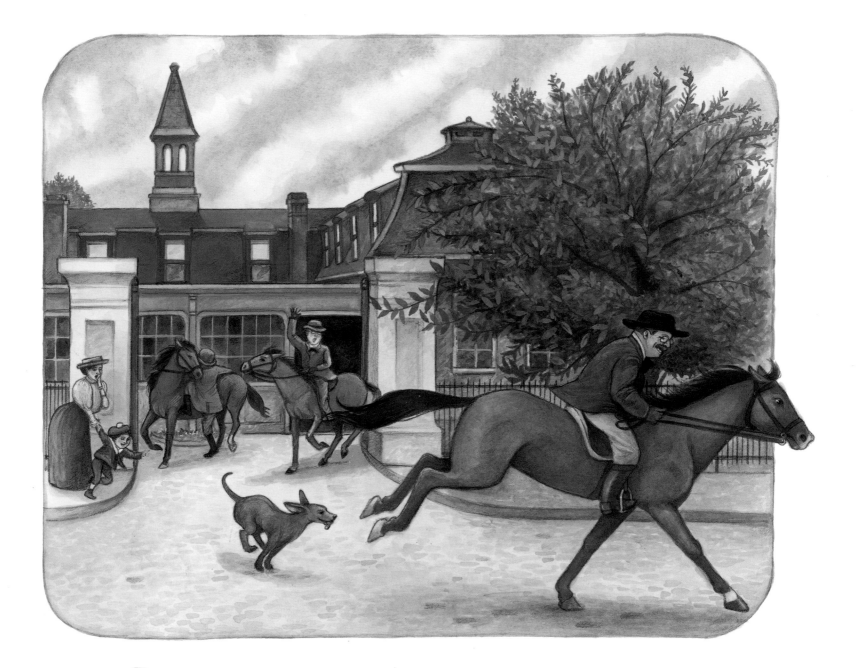

President Theodore Roosevelt mounted his favorite horse and shook the reins. He and Renown shot out the White House stable door. They galloped straight for the woods on their daily ride. As always, hooves pounded behind them. The President made sure that the Secret Service had to ride hard to keep up with him.

America's twenty-sixth president loved his busy job . . . except for one thing. He missed what he called the "strenuous life." He wanted to hike alone through the woods, whistling for birds. He longed to chop wood or hunt wild animals.

Most nights, he set aside time to read. Some of his favorite books were about nature. One evening in the White House, the President finished John Muir's newest book, *Our National Parks*. The author's descriptions of California's Yosemite National Park fascinated the President. He tried to picture the three-thousand-foot-high walls that surrounded Yosemite Valley. Besides all the waterfalls, there were granite boulders bigger than buildings, with names like Half Dome and North Dome. Distant mountain peaks soared over ten thousand feet into the sky.

Muir's nature essays clearly indicated a man with strong opinions about land preservation. Roosevelt enjoyed lively discussions. It would be exciting to talk with the country's best-known expert on conservation *and* explore Yosemite.

But why couldn't he? He was the President of the entire United States, wasn't he?

The President picked up his pen. He wrote so fast that his spectacles danced to the tip of his nose.

Dear Mr. Muir,
I am coming West. I want to go camping with you and no one else. . . .

In his letter, he explained that he had already decided to take a fact-finding trip in the spring of 1903. Roosevelt had never seen the far West, and he was eager to meet the people and learn about the natural resources, such as minerals, trees, and water. This visit would help the President make better decisions about the region in the future.

Roosevelt wrote Muir that he would first visit Yellowstone National Park. After seeing the Grand Canyon and Arizona, he would come to California by train. To wrap up his trip, the President asked Muir to guide him through the Yosemite area. While camping and avoiding dignitaries, they could talk.

The President grinned as he stamped his official seal on the back of the envelope. Camping sounded bully! He especially wanted to see California's giant sequoia trees, the largest living things in the world. Four whole days in the Yosemite wilderness! The President felt giddy with excitement.

He would have to get some Western clothes.

Months later, the President's special train sped southeast across California, from Oakland on the coast, to reach the tiny town of Raymond, at the end of the railroad line.

"I am dee-lighted to meet you," President Theodore Roosevelt said, pumping Muir's hand up and down.

Soon Roosevelt and Muir were escorted with the rest of the presidential party in stagecoaches some thirty miles up through the foothills of the Sierra Nevada into the Yosemite wilderness. The two men stood in the Mariposa Grove of Big Trees in front of the Grizzly Giant, one of the largest giant sequoia trees in the world. On either side of Muir and Roosevelt, important men, including George Pardee, governor of California, posed for the cameras. *Poof!* Burning white flash powder blinded them.

Roosevelt smiled his famous toothy grin for the cameras. Reporters would write about the Grizzly Giant and the other trees in this grove. But they wouldn't have much else to write about because the President didn't plan on seeing them any time soon!

The President announced that he was "prepared to go into the Yosemite with John Muir. . . . I want to drop politics absolutely for four days. . . ." He punched his fist in his hand for emphasis.

Everyone roared with disappointment. But there was no arguing with the strong-willed leader of the United States. He waved away the reporters. All the dignitaries climbed into their stagecoaches. Thirty cavalrymen mounted their dapple-gray horses. They saluted their President.

Finally, the President even ordered his Secret Service men to stay away.
Spurs jingled and leather creaked. The President watched everyone head down
the zigzagging road to the nearest town.

Three men waited with the pack animals and gear. They were under the
watchful eye of government ranger Charlie Leidig. Charlie's family ran a hotel in
Yosemite Valley, where he had lived and worked his entire life. He was the perfect
man to be in charge of the day-to-day details of the camping trip.

Centuries-old giant sequoia trees surrounded Roosevelt. He reached out
to touch the cinnamon-colored bark of the Grizzly Giant. It felt spongy.
Twisted tree limbs reached toward the sky, so heavy they didn't even sway in the
afternoon wind.

Deep in the forest, a squirrel chattered. Then a bird sang.

The President whistled back, hoping to draw out his first Yosemite bird.

A robin dropped from a branch and pushed debris about on the forest floor.

Roosevelt pulled out a pocket-sized notebook he always carried. He wrote down "Yosemite Wilderness, May 1903, robin."

Then the President sucked in a deep breath of brisk mountain air. "Now this is bully!" he shouted. "Boys, let's build a campfire."

13

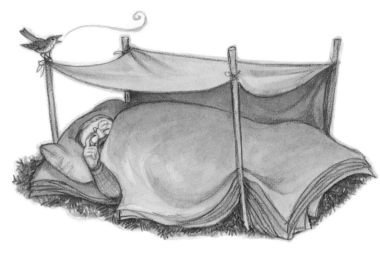

When Roosevelt woke up the next morning, he recognized the "wonderful music" of a hermit thrush, one of his favorite birds.

The President was starving! He wrestled the fry pan from Charlie. Before long, bacon-scented smoke drifted into the forest. Then the President scrambled six eggs beside the slab of bacon.

He ate a huge breakfast, happy to be away from the White House cooks who fussed over his diet.

After nibbling on a crust of bread, John Muir picked up a sequoia cone. He shook it. Tiny dark seeds, much smaller than snowflakes, spilled out. Muir explained that, from just one seed, the Grizzly Giant had sprouted about two thousand years earlier. Other trees in the grove were almost as old. Many were hundreds of years old. Sequoias, Muir added, grew on the western slopes of the Sierra Nevada, but nowhere else in the entire world.

Roosevelt's eyes widened with surprise.

Sequoia cone

Moments later, Muir scrambled up a nearby sequoia tree stump like a mountain goat. *He is pretty spry for a sixty-five-year-old*, Roosevelt thought.

The stump's flat top was big enough to hold a dozen men or more. Muir yelled that it had taken several days to saw down this tree. When it crashed to the ground, the tree shattered into splinters. Sequoia wood was of little use, except for fence posts. But lumbermen still continued to cut these trees.

The President shook his head in disgust. How could anyone cut a tree that had been growing for so long? For fence posts! What if future generations never saw a giant sequoia tree?

He and Mr. Muir would have to chat about forest preservation, but later. It was time to go. Roosevelt swallowed one last cup of coffee, strong and hot, just the way he liked it.

His horse snorted and danced sideways along the trail. The President looked back. No one seemed to be following him! Had he truly escaped the ever-watchful eyes of his Secret Service men?

Hours later, the two men arrived at Glacier Point, with its spectacular views. Swirling wind tried to take the President's hat as Roosevelt and Muir inched out onto Overhanging Rock at the tip of Glacier Point.

Yosemite Valley lay three thousand feet directly below them. The Merced River, a curving ribbon of gray-blue, flowed through the green valley floor. Rock walls, interspersed with waterfalls, ringed the valley. Muir pointed out Upper and Lower Yosemite Falls, with mist rising from below, and the sheer face of Half Dome. The rugged-looking high-mountain country stretched beyond.

For a change, Roosevelt was speechless.

Suddenly, reporters appeared, interrupting with questions and calls of "Mr. President. Mr. President." The wind picked up their words and blew them away. The President's jaws snapped shut. Where had they come from?

Once again, people and cameras surrounded him. The President was angry—very angry. He marched to his horse. "Boys, keep them away from me," Roosevelt barked at the Secret Service, glad for once that they were lurking nearby.

How could he rough it with a crowd around him?

At sunset, Roosevelt and Muir picked a new camping spot. The President grabbed an ax and insisted on starting the fire. Sweat flew from his forehead as he chopped firewood. Before long, a sizzling-hot campfire glowed in the dark. And once again, Roosevelt took the fry pan from Charlie.

While the President chewed his way through a platter of steak and fried potatoes, Muir spoke of the need to provide "government protection . . . around every wild grove and forest on the mountains." He urged Roosevelt to set aside land, including the Mariposa Grove of Big Trees and the state-run Yosemite Valley, which they would visit the next day.

The President had never met anyone who talked as much, or as fast, about the importance of nature. In fact, Muir seemed to live on words, not food! As Roosevelt listened, he heard a noise in the trees above him. Was it a dreaded Secret Service man, guarding him in a tree? He listened again. Then he chuckled. In his notebook, the President wrote "owl."

Four to five inches of snow
covered them by morning!

"This is bullier yet! I wouldn't miss this for anything," the
President shouted, shaking snow from his blankets. He shaved
by the light of a roaring campfire, then trimmed and waxed his
moustache.

That morning, they followed a narrow trail that hugged the vertical
granite walls. It was late afternoon when the small, dust-coated group rode
into Yosemite Village, a cluster of tents and wooden buildings.

A waiting crowd cheered loudly and pressed forward, hoping to shake the President's hand. He dismounted.

"[Mr. Muir and I] slept in a snowstorm last night. This has been the grandest day of my life! One I shall long remember! Just think of where I was last night. Up there"—and with a sweep of his hand, he pointed to Glacier Point—"amid the pines and silver firs . . . and without a tent."

The President waved his hat. "Now, Mr. Muir and I will pitch camp near Bridalveil Fall!" He mounted his horse. It reared suddenly, legs pawing the air. Charlie stepped forward to push back the throng.

Tails swishing, the pack animals stood at the edge of the campsite. The air turned chilly after the sun set. Suddenly, a mule brayed. Twigs snapped. Suspecting that they had been followed, Charlie disappeared into the dark. He told hundreds of waiting admirers in a nearby meadow to leave because the President was very tired. "They went—some of them even on tiptoe, so as not to annoy their President," he later told Roosevelt.

As the moon came up, the President took off his shoes and rolled up his pant legs. Wading in the icy-cold stream, Roosevelt hollered to John Muir. He was "as happy as a boy out of school."

Then the two men lay on their mattresses of ferns and fir branches, still talking about the waste of natural resources. For once, the President mostly listened. He respected the mountaineer's advice on the importance of preserving land around the entire country.

Above them, El Capitan glowed in the nighttime light. The Merced River flowed softly; Bridalveil Fall thundered. And it was growing late. The President was tired. "Good night, boys!" he said. He burrowed under his blankets and fell asleep. For the third night in a row, he snored.

Too soon, though, sunlight streamed into the valley. The President's horse-drawn stagecoach brought his official party.

"It was bully," the President said, pumping John Muir's hand.

"I've had the time of my life!"

Roosevelt climbed into his stagecoach and leaned over. "Good-bye, John. Come and see me in Washington."

Then he motioned John to come closer. "Be patient. Congress may sleep through my long-winded speeches, but I promise to wake them up."

What a magical place, Roosevelt thought, gazing around one last time. He was glad he had come to Yosemite. He felt more alive than ever, thanks to his bully-good camping trip with John Muir. Once back in Washington, Roosevelt would be able to do "some forest good," as the old naturalist would say.

Roosevelt peered in every direction as his stagecoach circled the valley. He wanted to savor his memories of Half Dome, of sunlight washing over glacial rocks, Yosemite Falls roaring, of deer grazing, and the lingering smell of a Yosemite campfire. Then he waved one final good-bye.

Moments later, the President was gone in a cloud of dust.

Author's Note

President Theodore Roosevelt's 1903 Yosemite camping trip was daring and unusual. Except for those four very special days in the Yosemite wilderness, Roosevelt was always surrounded by the press, dignitaries, crowds of admirers, and the ever-vigilant Secret Service.

Following his camping trip with John Muir in May, President Roosevelt spoke on the steps of California's Capitol Building.

> I have just come from a four days' rest in the Yosemite. . . . California possesses a wonderful climate, a wonderful soil. . . . the water supply cannot be preserved unless the forests are preserved. As regards some of the trees, I want them preserved because they are the only things of their kind in the world. . . . It would be a shame to our civilization to let them disappear. They are monuments in themselves. . . . We are not building this country of ours for a day. It is to last through the ages.

The President returned to the White House after visiting twenty-two states, two territories, and several national parks during his two-month-long tour of the West.

During his presidency, Roosevelt added 148 million acres to the existing forest reserves. He used his influence to help establish five new national parks and to create sixteen national monuments. One of the protected areas is Muir Woods National Monument (www.nps.gov/muwo), a tract of California redwoods named for Roosevelt's Yosemite companion. In 1906, both Yosemite Valley and the Mariposa Grove of Big Trees became part of Yosemite National Park (www.nps.gov/yose).

Roosevelt and Muir continued to correspond. In one letter, Roosevelt wrote Muir: "How I do wish I were again with you camping out under those great sequoias, or in the snow under the silver firs!"

Muir wrote back. "O for a tranquil camp hour with you like those beneath the sequoias in memorable 1903!"

But they never camped together again.

I hope that everyone will have a chance to experience the "strenuous life" in Yosemite National Park and visit its natural wonders: Glacier Point, Yosemite Valley, the Merced River, Bridalveil Fall, El Capitan, and the Grizzly Giant in the Mariposa Grove of Big Trees.

To write *Camping with the President*, I relied on my years of research. While preparing my juvenile biography, *John Muir, Wilderness Protector*, followed by *Giant Sequoia Trees*, I studied John Muir's papers at the Holt-Atherton Center for Western Studies at the University of the Pacific in Stockton, California. The staff at the Yosemite National Park Research Library and at the John Muir National Historic Site (www.nps.gov/jomu), his home in Martinez, California, also helped me find answers.

I used many significant primary sources. Some of the book titles are: *The Life and Letters of John Muir* by William Frederic Badè, Muir's literary executor; *Son of the Wilderness: The Life of John Muir*, the 1945 classic biography by Linnie Marsh Wolfe; works by Yosemite historian Shirley Sargent, including *John Muir in Yosemite* and *Dear Papa, Letters Between John Muir and His Daughter Wanda*; and *John Muir: A Reading Bibliography* by William and Maymie (also spelled *Mayme*) Kimes.

I reread many of John Muir's books, including *My First Summer in the Sierra, The Story of My Boyhood and Youth, The Yosemite,* as well as *John Muir in His Own Words: A Book of Quotations,* edited by Peter Browning.

I reviewed various Web sites devoted to Muir, including www.johnmuir.org and www.sierraclub.org/john_muir_exhibit.

Theodore Roosevelt was also a prolific writer of books and articles. A vast collection of his material is housed at Harvard University's Houghton and Widener Libraries in Massachusetts. I read Edward Renehan Jr.'s *The Lion's Pride: Theodore Roosevelt and His Family in Peace and War* plus his magazine articles about our twenty-sixth president. Reading Roosevelt's *Theodore Roosevelt: An Autobiography* and *Theodore Roosevelt's Letters to His Children* helped me understand this dynamic man. So did Kathleen Dalton's *Theodore Roosevelt: A Strenuous Life*; *The Rise of Theodore Roosevelt* by Edmund Morris; *Roosevelt the Explorer: T.R.'s Amazing*

Adventures as a Naturalist, Conservationist, and Explorer; and *The Bully Pulpit: A Teddy Roosevelt Book of Quotations,* both by H. Paul Jeffers. I also read *California Addresses by President Roosevelt.* On the Internet, I viewed Theodore Roosevelt: Icon of the American Century at www.npg.si.edu/exh/roosevelt, among other sites.

I visited Sagamore Hill National Historic Site in Oyster Bay, New York (www.nps.gov/sahi), where Theodore Roosevelt lived, as well as his rustic cabin, Pine Knot, in Keene, Virginia. Nearly every year, I spend time in Yosemite National Park. I have been to each of his three camping spots.

Only one eyewitness record of the camping trip exists. Charlie Leidig's internal park document "Report of President Roosevelt's Visit in May, 1903" is a sparse, four-page account written in third person. After studying John Muir and Theodore Roosevelt and reading Leidig's report, I wrote *Camping with the President.*

For young readers who want to know more about these two leaders, there are many marvelous books. I enjoyed *Theodore Roosevelt: The Adventurous President*, produced by the editors of *Time for Kids*; *The Remarkable, Rough-Riding Life of Theodore Roosevelt and the Rise of Empire America* by Cheryl Harness; *Theodore Roosevelt: Champion of the American Spirit* by Betsy Harvey Kraft; *John Muir: America's First Environmentalist* by Kathryn Lasky; and *John Muir: Magnificent Tramp* by Rod Miller. Find these titles and others at your public library.

—G.W.

About the Players

Theodore Roosevelt

Born in 1858 in New York City, Theodore Roosevelt suffered from severe asthma as a young boy. He became an avid reader and developed a strong interest in natural science, collecting bird nests, skulls, turtle shells, and much more. Thousands of items, including preserved animal skeletons and skins, became part of his "Roosevelt Museum of Natural History" on the fourth floor of the family home. Later, he donated this collection to the American Museum of Natural History (www.amnh.org).

Teddy's favorite books were about animals. He loved family trips to the Adirondacks in upstate New York and, later, to Maine. Both as a boy and as an adult, he enjoyed big-game hunting around the world. While at Harvard College, he studied natural history and joined the Nuttall Ornithological Club, America's first bird club. Even as a young man, Roosevelt had a remarkable way of describing the spirit of the wild and spacious land he loved so much.

After his first wife died in 1884, Roosevelt settled on his large cattle ranch in the Dakota Territory and spent his days outdoors. Since 1978, some seventy thousand acres as well as the Maltese Cross Cabin, Roosevelt's first home there, comprise the Theodore Roosevelt National Park (www.nps.gov/thro).

Roosevelt helped form the Boone and Crockett Club (www.boone-crockett.org) in 1887, a conservation organization for hunters who also wanted to preserve the natural world, and he wrote three books about his worldwide hunting experiences. Much later, Roosevelt wrote: "More and more, as it becomes necessary to preserve the game, let us hope that the camera will largely supplant the rifle."

Roosevelt held various public positions in New York City. Later, he became the governor of New York. Then Roosevelt was elected vice president of the United States. In 1901, President William McKinley was assassinated. At the age of forty-two, Theodore Roosevelt was sworn in as the president of the United States. He moved from his home at Sagamore Hill, in Oyster Bay, New York, to the White House with his second wife, Edith, and his children (www.whitehouse.gov/history).

The Secret Service, which was created in 1865 to deal with counterfeit money, changed direction in 1902, taking on the responsibility of protecting the president.

John Muir

John Muir was born in Scotland in 1838 but moved to the United States when he was eleven. On the family's wheat farm near Portage, Wisconsin, Johnny listened to birds singing in the woods and always found time to enjoy "Nature's glad wildness." By watching frogs in a pond, he taught himself how to swim and discovered an underwater world to study. At night, he invented things, including a bed that tipped him out when it was time to wake up.

Finally, Muir left home to explore "any place that is wild." He arrived in California just before his thirtieth birthday. Since he disliked cities, Muir fled San Francisco and walked east until he reached Yosemite Valley in the Sierra Nevada.

Muir often hiked alone for days or weeks in the mountains. At night he slept on a rock beside a stream or in a hollowed-out tree trunk. "Here, without knowing it," he later wrote, "we still were at school. . . . Nature streaming into us, wooingly teaching, preaching her glorious living lessons . . ."

He wrote magazine articles and books at his California ranch where he lived with his wife, Louie, and their two daughters. He farmed and wrote about the importance of preserving wilderness. Over the years, as a result of his writing, he became famous all around the world.

One of the happiest days of his life was on May 28, 1892, when he and his friends formed the Sierra Club (www.sierraclub.org). John Muir was elected the first president of what would become one of the most powerful environmental groups in the Western world.

About the Stage

Yosemite National Park is in California's most rugged mountain range, the Sierra Nevada, which lies about two hundred miles east of San Francisco. Today, the park is twelve hundred square miles in size. Yosemite Valley is seven miles long and, in some places, a mile wide. It was created millions of years ago by slow-moving glaciers that gouged out the granite rocks. As John Muir said, "No description of Heaven that I have ever heard or read of seems half so fine." There are grassy meadows, towering cliffs, canyons, rock domes, fast-moving rivers, waterfalls, glaciers, and much more.

The Mariposa Grove of Big Trees is in the southern end of the park. It is home to about five hundred giant sequoia trees, the largest of all living things. The Grizzly Giant, one of the oldest living sequoia trees in the world, is still growing!

sequoia cone

Acknowledgments

Many years ago, I had the honor of meeting John Muir expert Mayme Kimes. She and her husband, William Kimes, spent a lifetime collecting manuscripts, books, art, and other memorabilia by and about Muir. Over the years, Mayme and I became friends. Mayme died in 2002, and this book honors her remarkable spirit.

Thanks go to John and Marge Hawksworth, retired forest service employees, who watched over the Nelder Grove of giant sequoia trees near Oakhurst, California, for decades. My family camped there and absorbed sequoia and forest ecology from John and Marge. We often hike to the Hawksworth sequoia tree, named in memory of them. Appreciation goes to Roger Leclere, a former Colonial Williamsburg executive, who told my family stories about Theodore Roosevelt when he showed us Pine Knot, the president's rustic vacation home in Virginia.

Special thanks go to two readers, Harold Wood, chair of the Sierra Club John Muir Education Committee and Web master for the organization's John Muir site, and to Edward Renehan Jr., Theodore Roosevelt expert and author.

Yosemite National Park's librarian, Linda Eade, has helped me on my various Muir-related book projects. With the help of Yosemite National Park ranger and Buffalo Soldier expert Shelton Johnson, I was able to confirm that African American soldiers stationed in the park in 1903 cleared trails for this trip and perhaps even greeted Roosevelt and Muir at the Mariposa Grove of Big Trees. As a result of the dedicated work of Steve Medley (1949–2006), longtime director of the Yosemite Association (www. yosemite.org), many more families are learning about and enjoying this national park.

Authors Beverly Gherman (*Ansel Adams: America's Photographer*); Elizabeth Koehler-Pentacoff (*John Muir and Stickeen: An Alaskan Adventure*); and Donnell Rubay (*Stickeen: John Muir and the Brave Little Dog*) read my manuscript and gave me their helpful comments, big and small. So did my wonderful and patient agent, Karen Klockner. Thanks go to my editor, Carolyn P. Yoder, who helped launch my writing career when she was editor in chief of *Cobblestone* magazine.

To my first and last reader, Bill Wadsworth, thank you always.

—G. W.

Source Notes

Linnie Marsh Wolfe, *Son of the Wilderness: The Life of John Muir* (Madison: University of Wisconsin Press, 1978):
 Page 7: "Dear Mr. Muir …" (p. 290)
 Page 9: "I want to ..." (p. 290)
 Page 13: "Now this …" (p. 291)
 Page 20: "This is bullier …" (p. 292)
 Page 21: "[Mr. Muir and I] slept …" (p. 293)
 Page 22: "as happy …" (p. 291)
 Page 24: "I've had the time of …" and "Good-bye, John …" (both p. 293)

Theodore Roosevelt, *California Addresses by President Roosevelt* (San Francisco: California Promotion Committee, 1903):
 Page 9: "prepared … Muir" (p. 124)
 Page 26: "I have just come …" (pp. 139–140)

H. Paul Jeffers, *Roosevelt the Explorer: T.R.'s Amazing Adventures as a Naturalist, Conservationist, and Explorer* (Lanham, MD: Taylor Trade Publishing, 2003):
 Page 14: "wonderful music" (p. 113)

Peter Browning, editor, *John Muir in His Own Words: A Book of Quotations* (Lafayette, CA: Great West Books, 1988):
 Page 19: "government protection …" (p. 52)
 Page 29: "Here, without knowing it …" (p. 68)

Shirley Sargent, *John Muir in Yosemite* (Yosemite, CA: Flying Spur Press, 1971):
 Page 21: "Just think of where …" (p. 35)

Charlie Leidig, "Report of President Roosevelt's Visit in May, 1903" (from archives of Yosemite National Park Research Library):
 Page 22: "They went …" (p. 3)

William Frederic Badè, *The Life and Letters of John Muir*, Vol. 2 (Boston: Houghton Mifflin, 1924):
 Page 24: "some forest good" (p. 413)
 Page 26: "How I do wish …" (p. 416)
 Page 26: "O for a tranquil …" (p. 420)

H. Paul Jeffers, editor, *The Bully Pulpit: A Teddy Roosevelt Book of Quotations* (Lanham, MD: Taylor Trade Publishing, 2002):
 Page 28: "More and more …" (p. 29)

John Muir, *The Story of My Boyhood and Youth* (Madison: University of Wisconsin Press, 1965):
 Page 29: "Nature's glad wildness" (p. 42)

John Muir, *The Yosemite* (New York: Century Company, 1912):
 Page 29: "any place …" (p. 4)

John Muir, *My First Summer in the Sierra*, (San Francisco: Sierra Club Books, 1988):
 Page 30: "No description of Heaven …" (p. 39)

All other quotes are created by the author based upon typical language of Roosevelt and Muir or paraphrased from a book or document listed in the back matter.